Marley and the Great Easter Egg Hunt

Text and art copyright © 2013 by John Grogan

Cover art by Richard Cowdrey

Text by Natalie Engel

Interior illustrations by Lydia Halverson
All rights reserved. Manufactured in the United States of America.
No part of this book may be used or reproduced in any manner whatsoever without written permission except
in the case of brief quotations embodied in critical articles and reviews. For information address HarperCollins
Children's Books, a division of HarperCollins Publishers, 10 East 53rd Street, New York, NY 10022.
www.harpercollinschildrens.com

Library of Congress Cataloging-in-Publication Data is available.
ISBN 978-0-06-212524-8

Typography by Joe Merkel
12 13 14 15   LP   10 9 8 7 6 5 4 3 2
❖

First Edition

From the #1 *New York Times* Bestselling Author John Grogan

Marley

and the Great Easter Egg Hunt

and Illustrator Richard Cowdrey

HARPER

An Imprint of HarperCollins Publishers

On the morning of the big Easter egg hunt, Main Street hummed as people made their way to the town square. Friends and families strolled down the street together, chatting and laughing. Everyone, it seemed, was happy to join in the fun.

But there was one family running at full speed, led by a galloping dog.

"Slow down, Marley!" ordered Cassie as she chased after her dog. But Marley wasn't slowing down. His tongue hung out of his mouth and his ears flapped wildly as he flew down the street. He wasn't sure what an Easter egg hunt was, but he knew he wanted to be in the middle of it.

Marley finally skidded to a stop in the center of the square.

"What do you keep under that fur," Daddy said, trying to catch his breath, "a jet pack?"

"Marley's just excited for the hunt to start," said Cassie. "He wants to find all the Easter eggs himself."

"Welcome," the mayor said, addressing the crowd. "This year, we've hidden a very special egg. It's big. It's huge. Why, it's . . . *eggstraordinary*!"

Marley's ears started wiggling.

"Whoever finds it is the winner of the Easter egg hunt," the mayor continued.

Marley's tail started thumping.

"But look carefully—the egg might be big, but it's not easy to find."

"Aarroooo!" Marley bellowed. He was going to find that egg!

"Now, let the hunt begin," said the mayor. "On your mark. Get set. Go!"

Marley was gone in a flash.

"Hey, wait for us!" said Cassie, giggling.

When Marley's family caught up to him, he was sniffing his way through the park. Mommy laughed. "Looks like Marley is on the trail!"

Marley sniffed to his left. He sniffed to his right. He sniffed and zigged and zagged all the way to a park bench. There, behind a high patch of grass, was a bright plastic Easter egg!

Marley nudged the egg out from behind the bench. But before he could roll it back to Cassie and Baby Louie, a tiny hand reached out and picked it up.

"Look," said a little girl. "I found one!"

Marley whimpered softly.

"Sorry, Marley," Cassie said. "Let's get the next one."

Marley spotted a bright yellow egg nestled between two tree branches. He shimmied his way up one branch, then the next, until he had reached the egg. He opened his mouth wide to pick it up—but his paw slipped! The egg fell out of the tree and into a little boy's basket.

"Hey, that was Marley's!" cried Cassie, but the boy was already running back to his family. Marley let out a whine.

Marley found a plastic egg beneath some flowers. He found one on top of a statue. He dug one out from the park sandbox. But someone else always picked up the egg before he could get it.

"Oh, Marley," said Cassie as she chased after him from place to place. "There are so many other kids here. Maybe we should try looking somewhere else?"

That gave Marley an idea. The mayor had said that the big, special egg might not be easy to find. That could mean it might not be in the park with all the other eggs!

"Arf! Arf!" barked Marley as he took off.

"Where's that crazy dog going now?" asked Daddy.

"Waddy cwazy," said Baby Louie.

Marley tore through the town square to the shops across the street. He stopped outside the market, pressing his paws and nose against the store window. There, in a huge display, were a dozen fresh eggs arranged in an Easter basket. Maybe one of them was the special egg!

Marley's family caught up to him just as he was pushing his way through the market doors. Cassie gasped as she realized what was about to happen. "Marley, no!" she yelled. But it was too late.

Where twelve eggs had once been were now broken shells, lots of yellow yolks, and one sticky, messy dog.

"Oh, Marley," groaned Mommy as Daddy apologized to the grocer and paid for the eggs. "You have to stop!"

But Marley didn't hear her. He was already out the door.

From outside the window, Marley could see the baker frosting something big and pink and purple. It had to be the eggstraordinary egg!

"Arf! Arf! Arf!" Marley barked happily as he bounded into the shop.

He ran fast, leaping high in the air, straight at the big, beautiful egg.

"Wait! Stop!" cried the baker.

BAM! CRASH! CRRRRRUNCH!

Marley looked around. He and the baker were on the floor. So was the giant cookie Marley had thought was the egg. It was broken into tiny bits, with purple frosting everywhere. Marley tore out of the bakery and bolted around the corner.

"Follow those purple paw prints!" shouted Daddy.

Cassie traced the paw prints all the way to the party supply store.
She hurried inside as fast as she could. But it was too late.

Marley had already torn through a large, egg-shaped piñata. Bits of colorful confetti stuck to his fur. Long, colorful streamers billowed out behind him as Marley darted past Mommy, Daddy, and Baby Louie toward the door.

Cassie chased after Marley. Mommy and Daddy chased after Marley. The grocer, the baker, and the shopkeeper chased after Marley. Kids and their parents stopped searching for eggs and instead joined the chase for Marley.

"Stop! Heel! Slow down! Enough!" they shouted. But Marley would not stop. He ran up and down the street and around and around the block. Yet no matter where he went, the special egg was still nowhere to be found.

At last Marley ended up back in the town square,
just in time to see the mayor getting up to speak.
"Ladies and gentlemen," said the mayor,
"the Easter egg hunt is over!"

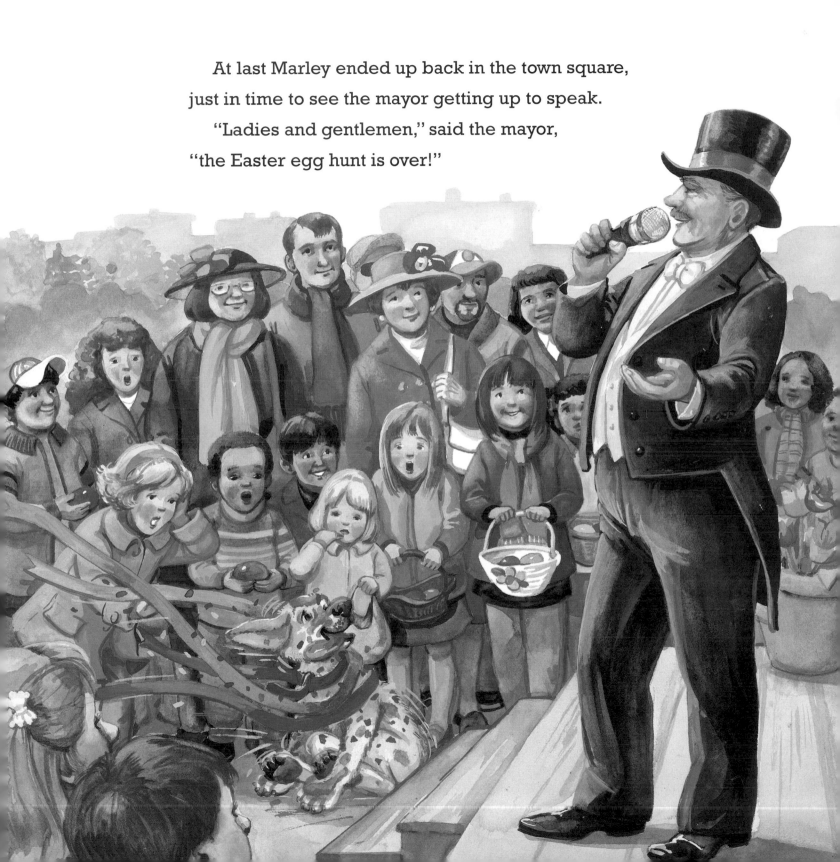

With a yelp Marley stopped in his tracks. Cassie, Mommy, Daddy, Baby Louie, the grocer, the baker, the shopkeeper, the kids, and their parents stopped, too. Marley lay down with a heavy sigh. He would not be the winner of the Easter egg hunt.

Cassie felt bad for Marley. "Oh, Marley, it's okay," Cassie whispered as she knelt down to pet him. "I wanted to find the egg, too."

"Did anyone find the big, special egg?" asked the mayor.

Marley and Cassie looked around. No one moved.

"Come now," said the mayor. "No one here has it? What about the young lady in the center of the audience—isn't that the large egg right next to her?"

The mayor was pointing at Marley. Covered in egg yolk, frosting, confetti, and streamers, Marley did look like a big decorated Easter egg.

"No, no," said Cassie. "That's not an egg. That's my dog!"

The crowd burst out laughing. Even the grocer, baker, and shopkeeper were smiling.

The mayor chuckled. "Bring him up here. I'd like to meet this Easter egg dog."
Cassie came up on the stage and told the mayor all about how Marley looked
everywhere for the special egg, with no luck.

"Well," the mayor said, turning to Marley, "you might not have found the big, special egg, but you certainly are this town's most *eggceptional* dog!"

The crowd roared. Marley thumped his tail and barked. He was so happy that he jumped all over the mayor to thank him. As he put his front paws on the mayor's shoulders, Marley accidentally knocked off the mayor's hat. Something big, round, and colorful was nestled inside.

"It's the special Easter egg!" cried Cassie. "Marley found it!"

"So it is," said the mayor. "Ladies and gentlemen, I present to you the winner of this year's Easter egg hunt."

Happy Easter, Marley!